For Charlemae and Joseph

JOHN HENRY

AN AMERICAN LEGEND

Story and Pictures by
EZRA JACK KEATS

SCHOLASTIC INC.
New York Toronto London Auckland Sydney

ISBN: 0-590-08344-9

13 12 11 10 9 8 7 6 5

Printed in the U.S.A.

A hush settled over the hills.
The sky swirled soundlessly round the moon.
The river stopped murmuring,
the wind stopped whispering,
and the frogs and the owls
and the crickets fell silent—
all watching and waiting and listening.
Then—the river roared!
The wind whispered and whistled and sang.
The frogs croaked, the owls hooted,
and all the crickets chirped.
"Welcome, welcome!" echoed through the hills.

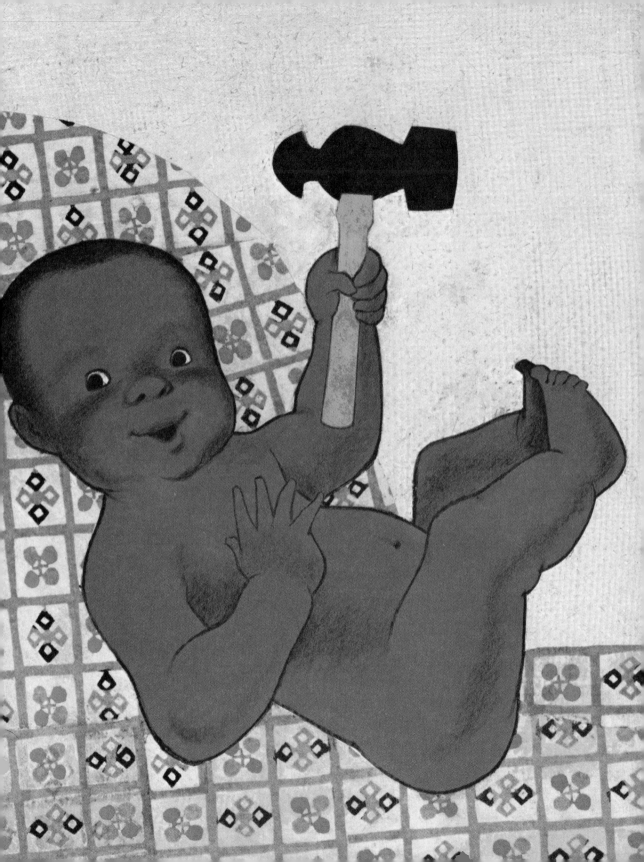

And John Henry was born,
born with a hammer in his hand!

"Bang! Bang! Bang!" rang little John Henry's hammer
through the cabin, as he crawled about.
"What's that rascal up to now?" his mother chuckled.
And before she knew it, he was big enough to help her
around the house.

As he grew up, he did a man's work with his father.
One day John Henry thought, "I'm taller and stronger than anyone around. It's time I went out into the world."
He said goodbye to his mother and father, and off he went.
He worked on farms and in cotton fields.
But all that was too tame.
So he got himself a job on a riverboat.

One stormy night the ship plowed through the darkness. Suddenly
the big steel rod that turned the paddle wheel broke. The wheel
stopped turning. Smash! went the rod through the bottom of the ship.
"Pump water!" shouted the captain. "Get to port before we sink!"
John Henry leaped to the paddle-wheel crank. He seized it,

pushed, grunted, and pulled. Slowly the giant wheel turned. With all his strength he kept it turning. "Lord Almighty, help us," someone whispered in that long, dark night. Day broke. They sighted shore and pulled into port. A thunderous cheer went up for John Henry!

John Henry felt a new excitement in the air. Men were talking
of railroads being built from the Atlantic to the Pacific.
"They're goin' to lay those tracks over rivers, across prairies
and deserts, and right through mountains."
"And through Indian lands and stampeding buffalo herds, and bad lands."
"Goodbye, boys," cried John Henry. "I'm goin' to swing me a hammer
on them beautiful new tracks!"

"My hands are just itchin' to hold a hammer again," John Henry said.
He tried one for size, and laughed. "It sure does feel fine."
How he drove those spikes, singing to the clanging of his hammer!
The men joined in, their voices singing, hammers ringing.
John Henry's gang was in the lead.
Day after day the tracks moved steadily westward.

Rising across their path was a sprawling mountain range.
Its snow-capped peaks reached high into the clouds.
"We'll have to tunnel through," said his friend, L'il Bill.
"It'll be awful dangerous. Could be cave-ins," someone put in.
"That suits me fine," said John Henry.
"Me, too," added L'il Bill.
"Here's how we'll do it, boys," the foreman called out.

"A couple of men'll drive a hole into the rock.
Then the powder men'll put dynamite into the hole and explode it.
The others'll cart the loose rock away.
We'll do this again and again until we have a tunnel right through
this mountain. And it's goin' to be a real big tunnel, boys.
Big enough for a giant locomotive pullin' one o' them long strings
o' trains. All right, boys, blast away!"

Deep into the mountain they worked. John Henry's singing
echoed through the tunnel. The powder men got ready to blast more rock.
They filled a hole with dynamite, put in a long fuse, and lit it.
"Run, men!" cried the foreman.
They all scrambled back, ready to dash clear of the blast.

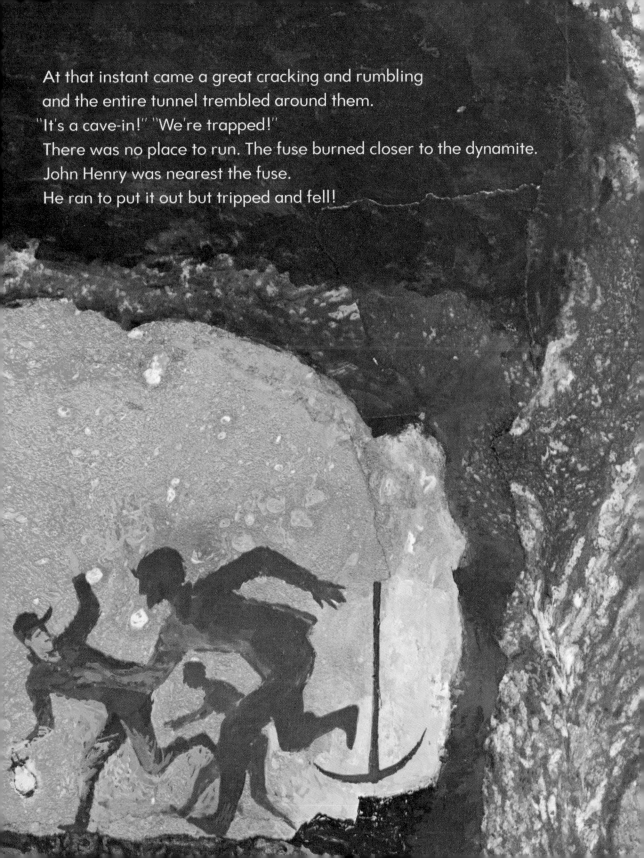

At that instant came a great cracking and rumbling
and the entire tunnel trembled around them.
"It's a cave-in!" "We're trapped!"
There was no place to run. The fuse burned closer to the dynamite.
John Henry was nearest the fuse.
He ran to put it out but tripped and fell!

"Oooh, I'm hurt bad," he groaned. "I can't get up."
The fuse burned farther out of reach. Others rushed toward it,
but they were too far away. Suddenly John Henry remembered—
he still had his hammer in his hand!
Down came the hammer—Smack! on the burning tip.

The fuse was out, danger past.
Sighs of relief filled the smoky tunnel.
"Whew! Help me up, boys," mumbled John Henry.
Clearing their way through the cave-in,
the men carried him to safety.

Down the tunnel came a group of men with a strange machine. "This is a steam drill. It can drill more holes faster than any six men combined," a new man bragged. "Who can beat that?"

John Henry stepped forward. "Try me!"
He and L'il Bill took their work places.
John Henry gripped his hammer. L'il Bill clutched his steel drill.
"Check the machine," came an order. A nervous hand fell on the switch.
In the dark both sides waited for the signal to start.
A hoarse voice counted, "One, two—

—THREE!"
The machine shrieked as it started.
John Henry swung his hammer. The crash
of steel on steel split the air!

Clang! Bang! Clang!
The drill got red-hot in L'il Bill's hands.
He quickly dropped it and picked up another.
Hiss! Whistle! Rattle!
Men frantically heaved coal into the hungry, roaring
engine and poured water into the steaming boiler.

Whoop! Clang! Whoop! Bang!
John Henry's hammer whistled as he swung it.
Chug, chug! Clatter! rattled the machine.
Hour after hour raced by.
The machine was ahead!
"Hand me that twenty-pound hammer, L'il Bill!"
Harder and faster crashed the hammer.
Great chunks of rock fell as John Henry ripped
hole after hole into the tunnel wall.
The machine rattled and whistled and drilled even faster.
Friends doused John Henry and L'il Bill with cold water
to keep them going.

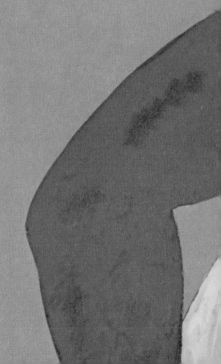

Then John Henry took a deep breath.
He picked up two sledge hammers, and sang:

"Ain't no hammers
Strike such fire,
Strike like lightning, Lawd,
And I won't tire!

"Hammers like this, Lawd,
There's never been!
I'll keep swingin' 'em, Lawd,
Until we win!"

John Henry swung both mighty hammers—faster and faster.
He moved so fast the men could see only a blur
and sparks from his striking hammers.
His strokes rang out like great heartbeats.

At the other side of the tunnel the machine shrieked, groaned
and rattled, and drilled. Then all at once it shook and shuddered—
wheezed—and stopped. Frantically men worked to get it going again.
But they couldn't. It had collapsed!
John Henry's hammering still rang and echoed through the tunnel
with a strong and steady beat.

Suddenly there was a great crash.
Light streamed into the dark tunnel.
John Henry had broken through!
Wild cries of joy burst from the men.
Still holding one of his hammers, John Henry stepped out
into the glowing light of a dying day.
It was the last step he ever took.
Even the great heart of John Henry could not bear
the strain of his last task.
John Henry died with his hammer in his hand.

If you listen to the locomotives roaring through
the tunnels and across the land, you'll hear them singing.
Singing of that great steel-driving man—John Henry.

Listen!